ARCTIC SPRING

By Sue Vyner

Illustrated by
Tim Vyner

Viking

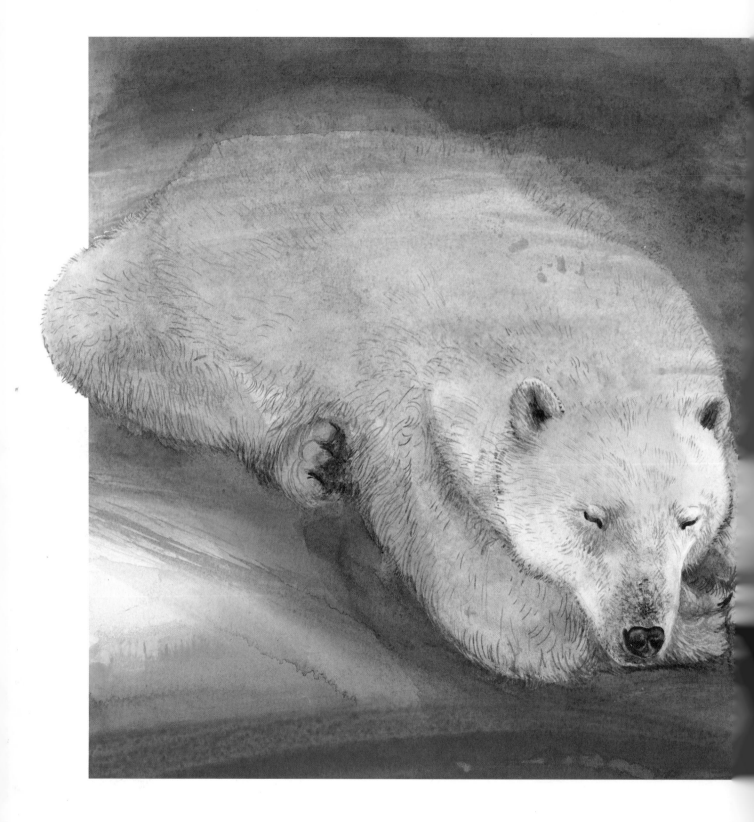

The polar bear is snug and warm, asleep in her den in the Arctic snow.

Outside a storm is raging. The wind howls and the snow swirls.

Later the polar bear wakes up. Now the long winter darkness is ending, so she climbs out of her den.

As she prowls in the snow she sees that the mass of ice is moving, drifting in the sea.

Back on land, something stirs. Long ears poke through the snow, bright eyes peer out.

The arctic hare wakes up because the winter darkness
has ended. He hops out of his hole.

The arctic fox, whose thick white fur blends into the snow, is awake too.

He is hungry after the long winter.
The hare quickly hides and the fox slinks by.

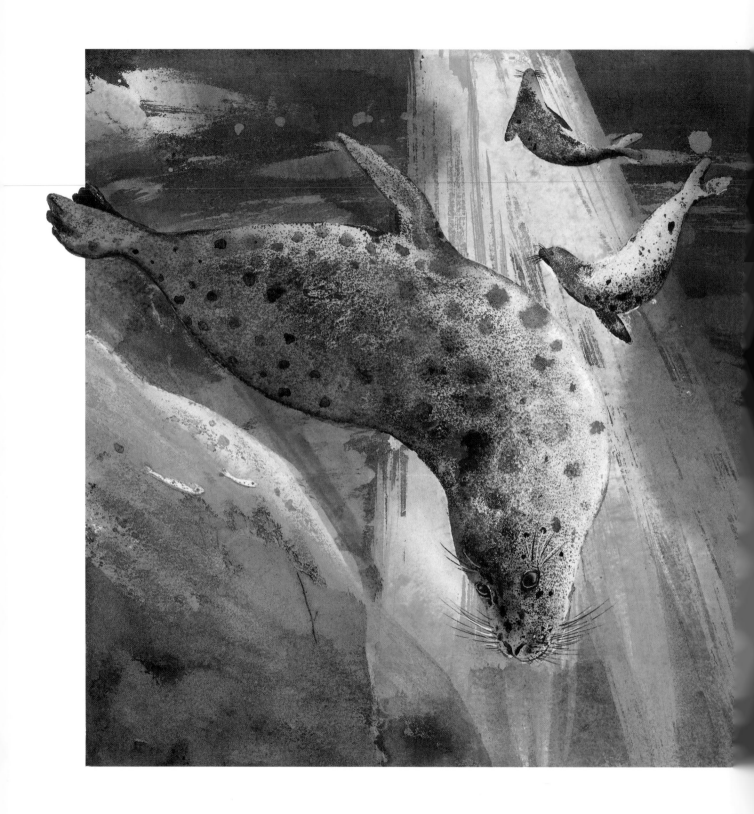

Sunlight filters through the ice to the cold water underneath, where the seals swim.

A seal finds an air hole in the ice and surfaces into the light.

Now the sun shines brightly.

Spring has come to the Arctic.

Out at sea, sunshine bathes the drifting ice
as the birds return.

A long, thin spike sticks out of the sea. A narwhal has swum
back to the Arctic to feed.

Strong currents are pulling the drifting ice out to sea.
If it reaches warmer waters, it will melt.

The polar bear could swim back to the safety of land,
but she stays on the ice.

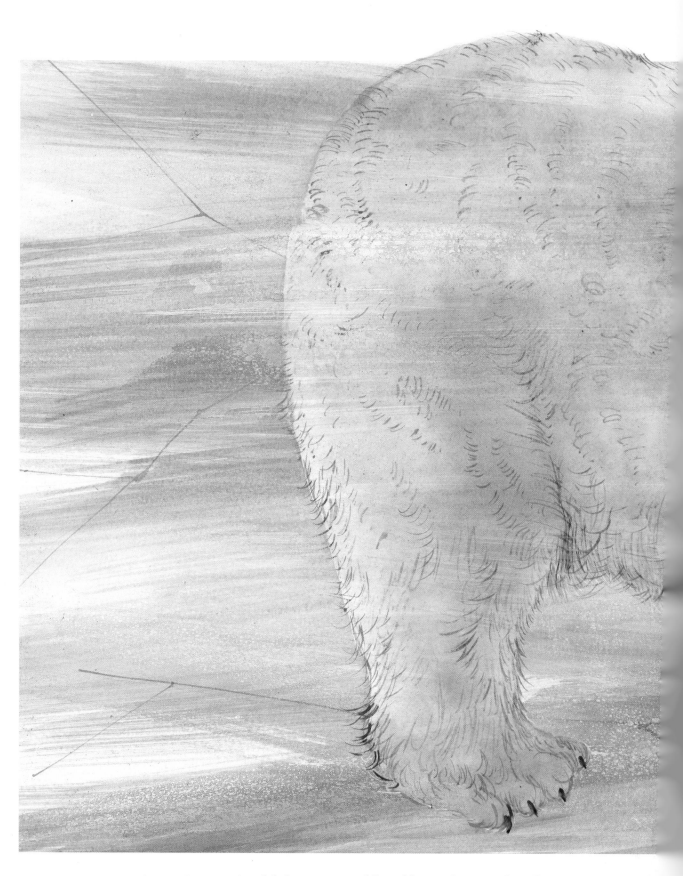

A spring wind blows and buffets the polar bear.
Pieces of ice break off and thunder into the sea…

…but she stands firm by her den.

When the wind drops, the ice has changed course.
Now it's drifting back toward land.

Crunch. With a colossal shudder, the ice collides
with the land. Then all is still.

The hare pauses to nibble the poppies that are
growing through the snow.

The fox stops to look for lemmings under the snow.

The seals bask in the sun and the narwhal feeds.

The birds screech and scream as they look for familiar places to build their nests.

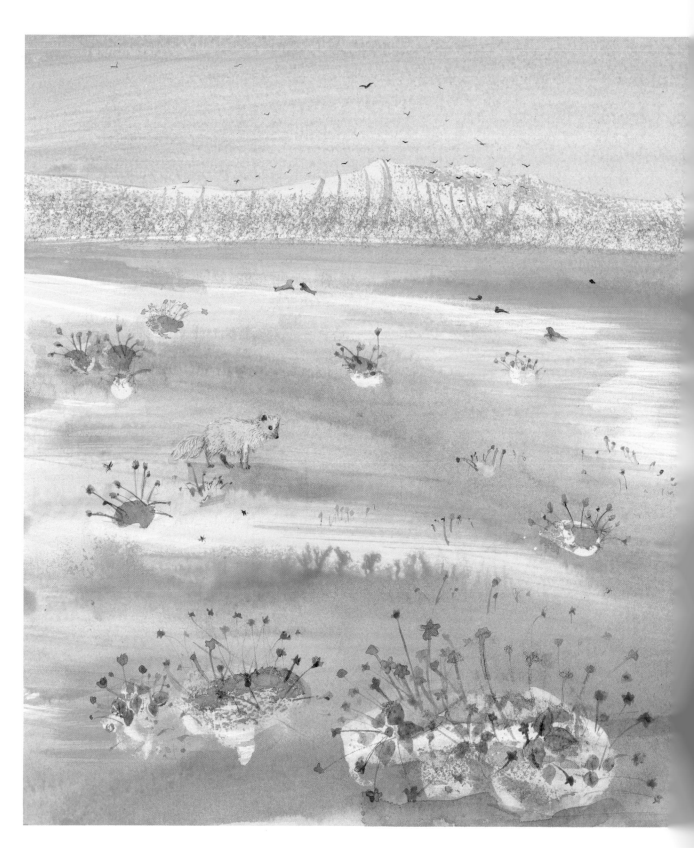

Everywhere the snow begins to melt.

In the warmth of the spring sunshine, the Arctic flourishes.

The snow shifts around the polar bear's den. Black, shining eyes blink and stare in the dazzling sun. It is a cub!

A second cub pushes out of the den, and the polar bear lumbers over to feed them.

Now at last the polar bear can leave her den. In the sunshine of the Arctic spring she sets off with her cubs, to find food and explore the ice and snow.

POLAR BEAR

The polar bear lives in the Arctic all year round. It has large paws with spiky hairs that help grip the snow and ice, and it is covered with a thick layer of fat for warmth. An excellent swimmer, the polar bear hunts seals. It is the most fearsome animal in the Arctic and the largest meat-eating creature in the world. This bear can weigh as much as half a ton and can grow to be taller than a man, even when it is on four paws. In winter the male wanders the ice, while the female gives birth to cubs in her den.

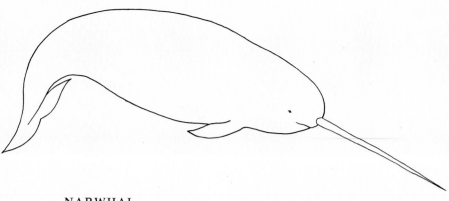

NARWHAL

The narwhal visits the Arctic in spring and summer. Families or "pods" feed on small fish at the edge of "ice floes" — floating sheets of ice. This large mammal weighs slightly less than 2 tons and is about 15 feet in length. It is the only whale in the world to have a tusk.

RINGED SEAL

The Arctic is home to many seals, including the ringed seal. This large mammal is over 3 feet in length and weighs around 145 pounds. Clumsy on land, it moves well in water, where it feeds on small fish such as arctic cod. When the seal needs to breathe, it often has to dig through the ice with its teeth and claws to make an air hole. In the spring these seals climb on to the ice and sunbathe for hours.

ARCTIC FOX

This small fox lives in the Arctic throughout the year. In summer it hunts birds and small mammals such as lemmings, storing away extra food for the winter, when it may even eat grass and berries. Like the arctic hare, this fox's fur turns gray or brown when the snow melts.

ARCTIC HARE

This hare lives in the Arctic all year round. It is the largest hare in the world, weighing 10 pounds and measuring nearly 2 feet in length. Its paws have special hairs that help it to grip the ice, and in winter it must dig through the snow to find food. The hare's white fur hides it from predators, but when the snow melts, its fur turns gray or brown.

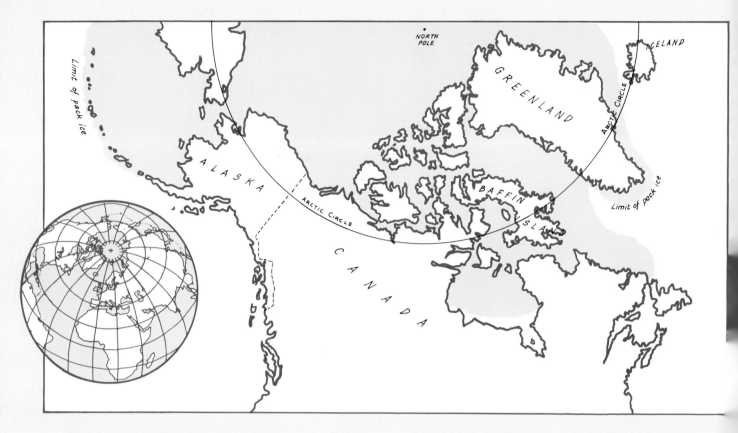

This map shows the Arctic. Most of the Arctic is sea, but around the North Pole, the extreme cold freezes the sea water into great pieces of ice that join together to form what is called "pack ice." This floating ice can be up to 20 feet in depth and can cover an area of over 1,865 miles wide. Ice also covers the northernmost regions of land within the Arctic Circle. Large chunks of ice often break off at the edges of these areas and float away until they melt in warmer waters — these are icebergs. Some of the Arctic lands are warm enough for the ice to melt in spring. These lands are the setting for this story.

VIKING
Published by the Penguin Group
Penguin Books USA Inc., 375 Hudson Street, New York, New York 10014, U.S.A.
Penguin Books Ltd, 27 Wrights Lane, London W8 5TZ, England
Penguin Books Australia Ltd., Ringwood, Victoria, Australia
Penguin Books Canada Ltd, 10 Alcorn Avenue, Toronto, Ontario, Canada M4V 3B2
Penguin Books (N.Z.) Ltd, 182–190 Wairau Road, Auckland 10, New Zealand
Penguin Books Ltd, Registered Offices: Harmondsworth, Middlesex, England
First published in Great Britain by Victor Gollancz Ltd., 1992
First American edition published in 1993 by Viking,
a division of Penguin Books USA Inc.

1   3   5   7   9   10   8   6   4   2

Text copyright © Sue Vyner, 1992
Illustrations copyright © Tim Vyner, 1992
All rights reserved

LIBRARY OF CONGRESS CATALOGING-IN-PUBLICATION DATA

Vyner, Sue.   Arctic spring / by Sue Vyner.
illustrated by Tim Vyner. — 1st American ed.   p. cm.
Summary: Spring in the Arctic brings new activity among the fox,
seal, and other animals, but the polar bear has a very good reason
for remaining firm by her den.
ISBN 0-670-84934-0
1. Polar bear — Juvenile fiction.   [1. Polar bear — Fiction.
2. Bears — Fiction.   3. Zoology — Arctic regions — Fiction.
4. Spring — Fiction.]   I. Vyner, Tim, ill.   II. Title.
PZ10.3.V98Ar   1993   [E] — dc20   92-32280

Printed in China   Set in Great Britain